Redworld is published by
Stone Arch Books, A Capstone Imprint
1710 Roe Crest Drive
North Mankato, Minnesota 56003
www.mycapstone.com

Library of Congress Cataloging-in-Publication Data
Names: Collins, A. L. (Ai Lynn), 1964– author. | Tikulin, Tomislav, illustrator.
Title: Asylum: refugees of Mars / by A.L. Collins; illustrated by Tomislav Tikulin.
Description: North Mankato, Minnesota: Stone Arch Books, a Capstone imprint, [2018] |
   Series: Sci-Finity. Redworld
Summary: When Belle Song goes to investigate a "meteor" which crashed near her family's
   Martian farm, what she finds is an escape pod holding two alien refugees fleeing a civil
   war; but while the politicians of Mars debate what to do about the Dirryn in general, Belle
   is determined to help these two refugees, particularly as one of them is about to give
   birth — even if helping means hiding them from her own parents.
Identifiers: LCCN 2017035490 [print] | LCCN 2017039194 [ebook] |
   ISBN 9781496558909 [eBook PDF] | ISBN 9781496558862 [library binding: alk. paper]
Subjects: LCSH: Extraterrestrial beings—Juvenile fiction. | Refugees—Juvenile fiction. |
   Secrecy — Juvenile fiction. | Families—Juvenile fiction. | Friendship—Juvenile fiction. |
   Science fiction. | Mars (Planet)—Juvenile fiction. | CYAC: Science fiction. | Extraterrestrial
   beings—Fiction. | Refugees—Fiction. | Secrets—Fiction. | Family life—Mars (Planet)—Fiction. |
   Friendship—Fiction. | Mars (Planet)—Fiction. | LCGFT: Science fiction.
Classification: LCC PZ7.1.C6447 [ebook] | LCC PZ7.1.C6447 As 2018 [print] | DDC 813.6 [Fic]—dc23
LC record available at https://lccn.loc.gov/2017035490

Editor: Aaron J. Sautter
Designer: Ted Williams
Production: Kathy McColley

Printed and bound in Canada.
010813S18

ASYLUM
REFUGEES OF MARS

BY A.L. COLLINS
ILLUSTRATED BY TOMISLAV TIKULIN

STONE ARCH BOOKS
a capstone imprint

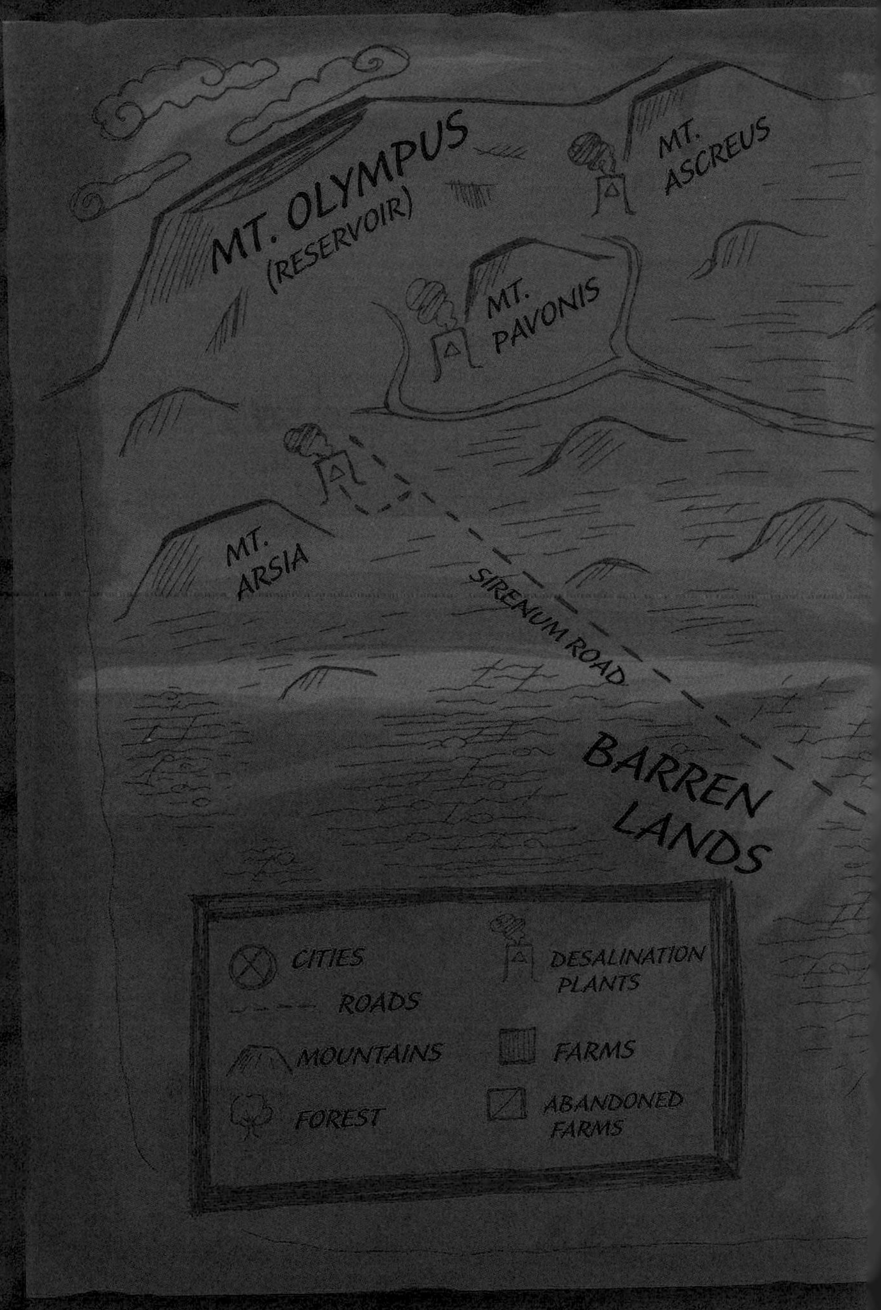
MT. OLYMPUS
(RESERVOIR)
MT. ASCREUS
MT. PAVONIS
MT. ARSIA
SIRENUM ROAD
BARREN LANDS
CITIES
ROADS
MOUNTAINS
FOREST
DESALINATION PLANTS
FARMS
ABANDONED FARMS

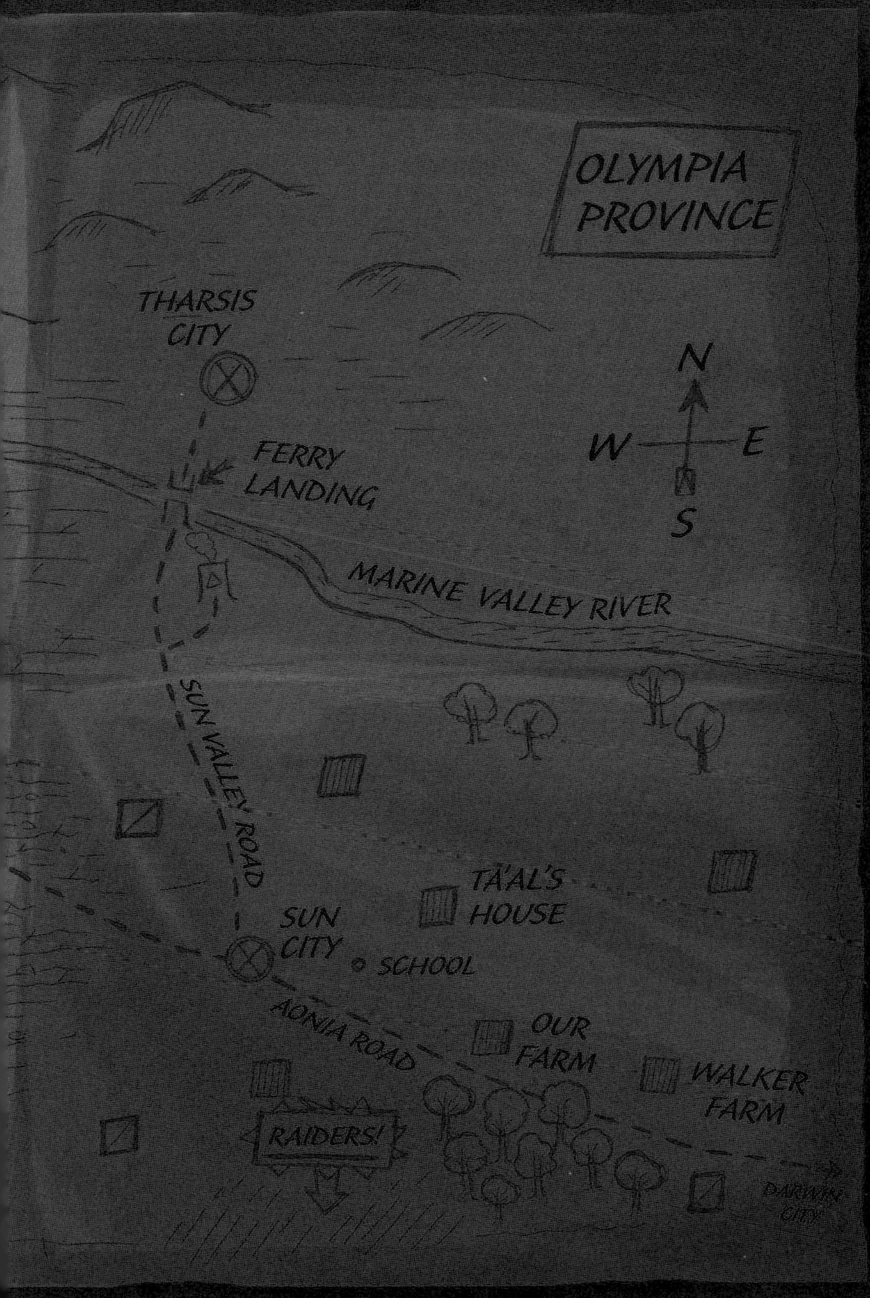

OLYMPIA PROVINCE
THARSIS CITY
N
W
E
S
FERRY LANDING
MARINE VALLEY RIVER
SUN VALLEY ROAD
TA'AL'S HOUSE
SUN CITY
SCHOOL
AONIA ROAD
OUR FARM
WALKER FARM
RAIDERS!
DARWIN CITY

Belle Song

Fourteen-year-old Belle can be headstrong and stubborn. Her curiosity and sense of adventure often get her into trouble. Still, she has a good heart and is passionate about fairness. She is fiercely loyal to her friends.

Yun and Zara Song

Belle's parents sometimes seem really strict. But Yun has a great sense of humor, which Belle both loves and is embarrassed by. Zara has a generous heart, which has taught Belle not to judge others too quickly.

Melody

Melody is an old model 3X Personal Home Helper android. She was given to Belle by her grandmother before she passed away. Melody is Belle's best friend and protector, and enjoys telling bad jokes to seem more human.

MAIN INHABITANTS

Lucas Walker

Lucas is Belle's neighbor and classmate. He is part Sulux and part human. Meeting new people is not easy for him. But once he knows someone, his adventurous side emerges. He is full of ideas, which sometimes gets him and his friends into trouble.

Ta'al

Ta'al and her family are Nabian, an ancient alien race from another star system. Born and raised on Mars, Ta'al is intelligent and curious. She enjoys exploring and adventure and quickly becomes Belle's closest friend on Mars.

Raider

Raider is a hybrid wolf-dog. These animals were bred to be tame pets, but some of them became wild. After Raider is rescued by Belle, he becomes a faithful and protective companion.

It is the year 2337. Life on Earth is very difficult. Widespread disease, a lack of resources, and a long war against intelligent robots has caused much suffering. Some Terrans, those who are from Earth, have moved to the Lunar Colony in search of a better life. But the Moon is overcrowded and has limited resources. Other families have chosen to move to Mars instead. With the help of two alien races — the Sulux and the Nabians — the red planet was transformed to support life nearly 200 years ago.

Yun and Zara Song and their daughter, Belle, moved to Mars about one Mars Cycle ago. Here they live as farmers. They work hard to grow crops and raise hybrid animals that are suitable for life on Mars.

Belle has just turned fourteen Earth-years old. She has made many friends and met several alien races. But on the night of her birthday, a major event leads her to meet the strangest aliens yet. Many people are afraid of the newcomers and their unusual abilities. But when Belle learns their sad history, she decides to do whatever she can to protect the alien refugees, and help them make a new home for themselves on . . .

RED WORLD

CHAPTER ONE
:BIRTHDAY:
WITH A BANG!

"Happy Birthday to you." Everyone sang at the top of their lungs. Belle blew out the fourteen candles on her cake. Her friends, family, and neighbors applauded. It was a perfect late summer's night. The sky was lit with stars, and one of Mars' moons, Phobos, was on the rise.

"Isn't it wonderful that even the heavens are celebrating your special day, Belle?" Mom said with pride in her eye.

"Oh, Dad," Belle sighed. Her dad was always trying to be funny, and it often embarrassed her. But tonight, his words felt like a great big hug.

Melody had put out blankets and chairs on their back lawn. The guests sat or laid back and chatted happily as they waited for the meteor shower to begin. Newscasters on RedVision had been talking about the event for days.

"There's one!" Lucas pointed. Belle's eyes followed his finger. She'd only just caught the end of the meteor's flight. It lasted less than a second.

"Quick, make a wish," Zara said, pointing out another meteor. Baby Thea squealed with delight.

"Do you believe in wish-making on a piece of rock hurtling through space?" Ta'al asked. Belle smiled. Her best friend was always the logical one.

"It's an Earth thing," Belle dismissed it with a laugh. It was hard to explain some human traditions to her Nabian friend. Perhaps they were too advanced a species to appreciate silly, Earth superstitions.

For the next few minutes, everyone was quiet as they watched for streaks of light in the night sky.

"I'm always looking in the wrong place when one appears," Belle said. She was getting a little frustrated.

"When you do see one, notice the tail of light," Melody said. The android was in her teacher mode. "It is due to the fact that a space rock creates friction as it enters the Martian atmosphere. The moment when a meteoroid crosses the sky, it becomes a meteor."

Belle's friends cried out when they saw another streak of light, but Belle had missed it again.

"I have a meteor joke," Melody said. "Would you like to hear it?"

"No!" A chorus of voices answered. Melody was famous for her bad jokes.

"Why does a moon rock taste better than a Mars rock?" Melody said, ignoring the kids.

"Do we even eat rocks?" Belle couldn't resist.

"Why does it taste better?" Ta'al asked Melody. She was too polite to ignore the android's attempt at humor.

"It's a little meteor." Melody looked at each face to see if they'd understood the joke.

All the kids groaned, except Ta'al, who rarely got the human puns.

"In this case *meteor* sounds like *meatier*," Belle explained to Ta'al.

Ta'al nodded, but didn't laugh.

"It's such a bad joke," Belle said.

"It is meant to be 'punny'," Melody answered.

Belle rolled her eyes. "I'm going to climb a tree," she said, standing up. She still hadn't caught sight of a meteor or its tail. "Maybe I'll have better luck up there."

Ta'al, Lucas, and Melody went with her. The kids climbed up the thick limbs of the giant apple tree at the end of the yard. Melody engaged her anti-gravity function, and simply floated upward. They stared out over the Songs' farm.

"What a beautiful night!" Belle exclaimed. She took in a deep breath, as if to inhale all of Mars' sky into her lungs.

"What's that?" Ta'al said suddenly. Everyone turned to look in the direction that Ta'al was pointing.

"It must be the comet everyone was talking about," Lucas guessed. "RedVision said the comet would bring on the meteor shower."

Belle hadn't realized that meteors or comets could burn so brightly. Instead of a bright white streak across the sky, this one was orange, as if it were on fire.

"That is very interesting," Melody said. Her eyes turned blue as she contacted the Martian wireless network. "There have been several reports about that sighting already. It does not appear to be a comet at all."

Belle stood up on her tree branch to get a better look.

"Please be careful, Belle," Melody warned. "I cannot save you from gravity."

In silence, the friends watched as the bright ball of fire arced across the sky.

"It's going to crash!" Lucas gasped.

"It's headed past the forest," said Belle, pointing toward the line of trees across the road from their house. "Luckily, the farms on that side are mostly abandoned."

They watched the fireball streak beyond the edge of the trees, disappearing on the other side.

"Not all of them," Melody corrected.

Before anyone could add another word, there was a loud explosion and the ground beneath them shook.

Some on the ground shrieked, Ta'al gasped, and Lucas swore as they all clung to one another. Belle grabbed the tree trunk and held on tight. Several seconds passed before the ground stopped shaking.

"Whoa! Was that a super-giant meteor?" Belle shouted to her parents, who appeared beneath their tree.

"I have no idea," Yun said, waving at her to get down.

Beyond the trees, a bright blueish-white light stretched high into the sky. Clouds of smoke also rose into the air.

"Let's go check it out!" Lucas was the first to climb out of the tree. The others followed.

On the ground, the adults were all talking intensely. They wanted to see what had landed too.

"If it crashed into a farm, someone's going to need our help," Paddy Walker said. Lucas' dad was always ready to help his neighbors.

Yun frowned. "I think you might be right."

"Our hover-wagon is ready to go," said Fa'erz, one of Ta'al's parents. Unlike humans, Nabian children had three parents.

Belle, Ta'al, and their families jumped into the Nabians' wagon. Behind them, the rest of the guests were getting into their own transports. Because the crash site was on the other side of the forest, they had to go the long way around to get to it.

A short while later, He'ern, Ta'al's father, parked the wagon near the crash site and everyone got out. The first thing Belle noticed was the stench. She could barely breathe in the hot, smoky air. She pulled her collar up over her nose.

Yun placed his hand on Belle's shoulder. "We shouldn't get too close," he warned.

Belle walked by her dad as they approached the giant crater caused by the crash. Whatever landed here had created a giant hole in the ground. Trees that hadn't been burned up were singed with black soot. Some were still on fire. The air itself felt as if it was melting from the heat. Everything before Belle's eyes was black.

Except for a glowing object . . . right in the middle of the crater.

No one spoke for the longest time. They just stared in disbelief.

"That's no meteor," Paddy said with awe. He didn't even say it in his usual loud voice. This was more like a loud whisper.

No one could believe their eyes. In the middle of the crater was a beautiful, glowing blue ball, about the size of a hover-wagon. It was encased in what looked like vines made out of gold.

"It's so shiny!" Belle exclaimed.

"It is definitely not naturally occurring," Melody said. Her eyes were switching from blue to green to red. She was trying to find out more information, while also reporting the incident to the authorities.

The heat from the crater grew stronger. Finally, Yun decided they should all head home until the authorities could investigate. "It might be radioactive," he said, pulling Belle away.

As they headed back to their transports, Belle couldn't help but look back. It was the most beautiful thing she'd ever seen. She had to find a way to come back and examine it herself.

Sol 166, Summer/Cycle 106

Well! My party ended with a bang!
Whatever that thing is, I want a closer look. Lucas and Ta'al said it wasn't anything they'd ever seen or heard of before. I'm pretty sure it's an alien object. What if it's from a brand-new alien race? What if they're really huge and this is one of their toys? Or maybe they're so tiny that the object is their entire world.
Dad thinks it could be dangerous though. He made me promise not to go near it until the authorities check it out. But I REALLY want to see it up close.

CHAPTER TWO
:REFUGEES:

"I don't understand why it's taking the authorities so long," Belle complained as she, Lucas, and Ta'al walked home from school. "It's been a week since that object crashed here."

"Scientists say the ball is definitely some unknown alien technology," Lucas said. He always spoke as if he had all the knowledge in the world. "I heard it on RedVision news last night."

"We all saw it," Belle said, exasperated. "I could've told the scientists that. I just can't believe that after all this time, they don't have anything new to say about it."

Ta'al was being very quiet, which made Belle think she knew something. Belle gave her a gentle nudge.

"I wasn't supposed to hear about this," Ta'al said. Her eyes were as gray as a stormy day. "I heard my parents talking last night. There's a big meeting happening in Utopia with all the government leaders."

"What's the meeting about?" Belle asked.

"Something about the *talazin parthenax* . . . I mean, refugees?" Ta'al said uncertainly. "The blue ball has something to do with them."

They'd reached the place where the path split into two. Ta'al would take one path to her house, and Belle and Lucas would take the other. But no one moved.

"What's a refugee?" Lucas asked.

"A refugee is someone who is fleeing their own world because it's too hard to live there anymore," Ta'al explained. "I heard my mother say that these refugees are a new race of aliens that no one's met yet. They might want to live here on Mars too."

"They can't just show up and start living here," Lucas said. He puffed out his chest, ready for an argument.

"Why not?" Belle said. "If they're in trouble, they need to live somewhere that's safe. Mars is pretty safe."

"I don't know much more," Ta'al said. "I was supposed to be in bed asleep, and I didn't like listening to my parents in secret."

Belle laughed. Her best friend always followed the rules. It was one of the things Belle liked about her. But Belle would have had no problems eavesdropping on her parents. Especially if it concerned new alien visitors.

Ta'al waved and began down the path to her home. Belle was about to head home too when she noticed that Lucas hadn't moved. He looked like he was concentrating on something rather unpleasant.

"Come on, Lucas," Belle called. "What are you doing?"

"I'm thinking," he said.

This could mean trouble, but Belle didn't mind. Lucas' ideas often led to interesting adventures. Even Ta'al turned back to hear what he was thinking about.

"We haven't seen the ball since the night it crashed," he said with a grin. "Why don't we go see it out for ourselves?"

"You *know* why," Ta'al said. "Because our parents told us not to."

"But it's been a whole week," Belle said. "I want to see it again, especially in the daylight."

A few minutes later the three friends were running down the path to Belle's house. They climbed over the Songs' back fence and dropped their school bags in the above-ground portion of the house. Belle's wolf-dog, Raider, was waiting for her. He barked happily and jumped up to lick her face.

"Come on, Raider," Belle said, breathlessly. "We're going to the crash site. But it's a secret, so no noise."

Raider seemed to understand. Without another bark, he followed them as they headed out to the forest across the road. The forest had become very familiar to them, so getting through it was easy. They ran quickly, dodging and jumping over roots and vines, not tripping even once.

They stopped at a clearing that looked down upon the crash site. Everything looked the same, yet different from that first night. The ground was still scorched and black, and several trees had all their leaves burned off. Their blackened branches stretched into the sky. In the middle of the crater, the alien ball still glowed a beautiful blue and gold. But now there was a large laser fence surrounding the object, and Protectors stood guard at its four corners. There were also people everywhere!

"It's become a tourist attraction," Ta'al said. She sounded upset. Various Martians were milling around outside the fence, taking holo-images with their devices.

"Some of those people look like scientists," Belle observed. She pointed to the people inside the fence, closest to the alien ball. They were in bright orange body suits, with a clear panel at their faces. They each carried some equipment, and a few were prodding at the object.

"They're in hazmat suits," Lucas said. "They must think the object is giving off radiation, or germs, or something."

"So why would they allow tourists?" Ta'al asked.

"We were quite close to it after it landed, and nothing's happened to us," Belle said. "I don't think it's dangerous. The scientists are just being overly careful."

"Poking it like that is asking for trouble," Lucas said with a frown. He squinted at the object.

"Let's go down there," Belle said. Before the others could disagree, she and Raider were already halfway down the hill.

The closer they got, the more Raider slowed down. The hair on his back began to stand on end. He whined.

"What's the matter, Raider?" Belle said, wishing she could understand her dog. "It's all right. I'm here."

Raider lagged behind Belle and her friends as they approached the laser fence.

"It's too far away to see anything," Belle complained. "I wish we could get closer."

Raider started to whine loudly. He was attracting the attention of the other onlookers. He calmed down when Belle ran her fingers through his fur. Ta'al and Lucas went off to ask a nearby Protector some questions.

A Martian couple with holo-vid cameras walked past Belle and Raider. They smiled at her and turned away to take footage of the site.

"What do you suppose this object is?" the man asked his companion, raising his holo-vid camera over his head. "RedVision says it's related to the talks in Utopia. Maybe it's a gift to the people on Mars. Maybe it's their way of impressing us with their technology."

"But why crash it way out here?" the woman replied. "It makes them look pretty incompetent."

Then she gasped as if an idea had occurred to her. "What if they crashed it on purpose to make it look like an accident?" she asked. "What if this thing is a weapon? What if they're really here to invade and take over Mars?"

Belle leaned in closer to hear their conversation. She wanted to know what the man thought too.

"Nah. It's been sitting here for a week," he said. "If it were a weapon, wouldn't it have gone off already? I think it's a distraction, or a publicity stunt — to make us focus on the object more than the talks in Utopia."

The woman frowned. "Maybe. But there's something about all this that makes me nervous," she said.

The couple moved on, holding their cameras up to continue shooting footage of the site.

"The Protector won't tell us anything," Ta'al said, approaching Belle and Raider. "It's not very helpful."

"Yeah, all it would say was 'Only authorized personnel are allowed beyond the fence,'" Lucas said, imitating the robotic voice of the Protector. "At least we got to see the object. We should head home."

On the way back, Belle told her friends what she had heard from the couple's conversation.

"Whatever is going on, people are worried," she said.

"It better not be a weapon," Lucas said. "No one would want them here if it was."

"I don't think it is," Belle said. "That's no way to ask for help, or for a new home."

"I wonder how refugee issues are handled on Mars?" Ta'al said. "From what I've learned of Earth history, it's a topic that stirs up a lot of emotion."

"I've read about that too," Belle said. "But I think if they need help, we should help them as much as we can."

"But what if there are thousands of them? Or millions?" Lucas asked. He walked along with his hand in Raider's fur. "What if they take up so much space that there's none left for the rest of us? We could all get pushed into tiny living spaces and have to fight over food or water."

Belle rolled her eyes. Lucas' attitude didn't seem right to her. Surely, if Mars could help these aliens, they should. There was still a lot of space on the planet. Many areas hadn't yet been terraformed. And really, all the people on Mars were refugees in some way — whether they were running from something, or wanted a different life. She was about to say so to Lucas when she heard a familiar sound.

"There you are." Melody appeared ahead, ambling along the uneven ground. "I have been looking for you. You were meant to be home more than one hour ago."

"Sorry, Melody," Belle said. "We got curious."

"I see. Did you know that an old Earth saying states that curiosity tends to destroy pets? You are lucky that Raider is not a cat," she said, petting Raider on the head.

"What an odd thing to say," Ta'al said. "What does that mean?"

Belle laughed. "Melody's just trying to be funny. She totally made that up."

When they arrived back at the Songs' house, Lucas and Ta'al took off for home. Belle stayed outside, throwing sticks for Raider to fetch. But her throws weren't going very far, and Raider began to lose interest.

"A credit for your thoughts," Melody said, taking the stick from Belle and tossing it a great distance. Raider barked happily and took off as fast as he could.

"What?" Belle squinted into the sunshine, watching her dog run after the stick.

"Clearly your mind is elsewhere."

Belle told Melody about what she'd heard and how her friends had reacted to the idea of aliens moving to Mars.

"I mean, we were aliens too, just over a cycle ago," Belle said. "And no one made us feel unwelcome."

Melody's eyes turned blue as she searched the local network for information on the situation. "That is true," she said. "But we are only one family, not an entire race."

"What do you mean? An entire race?" Belle asked.

"The latest information from Utopia tells us that the object is indeed alien. These aliens are called Oirryn, from the star system Pergonae," Melody answered. "They say that their planet has been gripped by a civil war for many years."

"That's awful," Belle said.

"RedVision reports that the Oirryn have suffered the most, as one race among many," Melody continued. "In an effort to bring peace to their planet, the Oirryn were given a fleet of ships and asked to leave. They have come to ask Mars for asylum. It is a very strange situation."

"Wait. You mean they were kicked off their own planet?" Belle couldn't believe her ears. If this was true, then she felt Martians had to accept these poor aliens. "They must feel so hopeless. We have to help them."

"It is not a simple matter," Melody said. Raider dropped the stick at her feet and she threw it over the corral housing a few alpacas. "The Utopian authorities have no way to verify the Oirryn's story. Their star system is not within our range of communication. For all we know, they are the ones who started the war."

Belle's chest felt tight and hot, as if a fire were starting inside her. "How terrible to lose your home and then be suspected of lying. If they were unfriendly, they wouldn't pretend to need help. They would just take Mars for themselves. We should believe them."

"You are young," Melody said. "Your thoughts and emotions are still idealistic."

Belle glanced up at her android. "You are old," she said.

"And humans have a saying — with old age comes wisdom," Melody retorted.

Belle huffed. "So, does your wisdom tell you to suspect everyone who asks for help?"

"Well said, Belle." An alarm sounded on Melody's torso. "We should go inside now. Dinner is ready."

Belle fed Raider and settled him in the stable with their horsel, Loki. Then she followed her android into their underground home. She couldn't stop thinking about the Oirryn. Surely someone would believe them and give them a chance to build a new life on Mars — just like Belle and her family did when they first arrived.

Sol 173, Summer/Cycle 106

RedVision reported tonight that Oirryn ships are orbiting Mars as the talks continue in Utopia. I asked Mom and Dad what they thought the glowing object was. Mom thinks it could be a gift, but it crashed in the wrong place. Dad thinks it could be a probe of some kind that's taking readings about life on Mars. Melody can't find any more information. She thinks the authorities don't know what it is.

Bottom line? No one really knows.

As I look up at the night sky, I can't help wondering about the Oirryn's ships up there. Are they looking down on us, hoping for some compassion? Are they tired from the long journey? Maybe they're scared and hungry. I wonder if they have enough food? Do they even eat food? I can't help thinking about how awful they must feel having to leave their homes.

Raider just started howling outside, and wild dogs in the distance are echoing his howls. Dad's gone out to stop him. And now Melody has unplugged herself, and her eyes keep changing color. I wonder what's going on?

CHAPTER THREE

:FIRST CONTACT:

"Where is he?" Belle cried, throwing open the stable doors. Loki grunted at her, annoyed at the disturbance so late at night. But Raider's bed was empty and her dog was nowhere to be seen.

"He bolted as soon as I opened the door," Yun said, yawning and rubbing his eyes. Then he pointed toward the forest. "He went that way."

Belle ran toward the farm gate, with Melody hovering close behind.

"We have to go after him," Belle said.

"He'll come back when he's ready," Yun said, closing the stable doors. "Maybe he's just gone to say hello to old friends."

"No!" Belle cried. "He could be in danger."

"It's too dark to go out there now," Yun said. "We can wait until morning. Now let's get back to bed."

Belle reluctantly followed her dad back to the house. But as soon as he disappeared into his room, she turned to Melody.

"I'm going after him," she said. She went to the closet and slipped on a heavier jacket.

"I am not surprised." Melody had mastered a sarcastic tone perfectly. But she had learned it was pointless to try to stop Belle once she made up her mind.

They snuck out as quietly as they could, and Belle took off toward the forest. She wasn't afraid of the dark, or the possible dangers. She had Melody, and the android's presence gave her courage.

They tracked Raider all the way to the crash site. As they came to the edge of the hill that looked down on the alien object, Belle noticed that something was wrong.

"The Protectors!" she cried. "Look, they've all been deactivated."

Sure enough, the Protectors, one at each corner of the laser fence, were standing completely still. Their usually alert red eyes were dark, and their heads hung awkwardly to one side.

"The laser fence has been disrupted as well," Melody observed. "And Raider is sniffing the object."

Belle ran down the hill toward her dog. "Raider, get away from there. Come here," she called.

Raider turned his head to look at her and whined. Then he went back to sniffing the object. As soon as Belle reached him, he placed himself between her and the object, forcing her to take a few steps back.

"What is it, boy?"

Before she could move in for a closer look, the blue ball began to glow. It lit up the entire area around them. Belle squealed. Her heart pounded loudly in her chest. Raider barked frantically. Melody's eyes turned red as she scanned the alien ball. A beam of light shot straight up from the top of the ball, lighting up the night sky. A strange whooshing sound seemed to come from within.

"Something's happening," Belle said, realizing that she was stating the obvious.

"I think we are about to make an important discovery," said Melody.

Before Belle could ask Melody what she meant, the ball began to vibrate. Within seconds, the alien object was a blur that blended in with the landscape. Belle felt as if her eyes had lost focus. She rubbed them and tried to look again. The ball seemed almost invisible.

And then, as suddenly as it had begun, the vibrations stopped. Everything was silent for several long seconds. Belle couldn't even hear her own heavy breathing. She stepped closer, unable to contain her curiosity.

The ball rumbled. The sound was coming from within. A line appeared on the blue ball, right in front of Belle. It went up along one side, then across and back down again, forming three sides of a rectangle. Bright white light seeped through the crack. Before Belle could take another breath, the crack opened. It was a door!

The door then seemed to vanish, leaving behind a rectangle of bright light. A shadow appeared in the middle of the light. At first it looked like a shapeless blob. Then it looked like Raider's shadow. Finally it came into focus, and Belle gasped.

"It's a girl!" She half-whispered, half-cried out.

The girl stepped out of the blue ball. She looked human! She had a head with two eyes, a nose, and a mouth. She had two arms and two legs, just like Belle.

"Hello?" Her voice was like an echo. It sounded both light and eerie in the darkness. But her face was kind — her dark hair and light-colored eyes sparkled in the blue light. As she approached Belle, she stretched out both hands. "I mean you no harm. Will you be my friend?"

That was the strangest introduction Belle had ever had. But for some reason, Belle liked this girl immediately.

"My name is Belle," she said. "Do you have a name?"

The girl tilted her head to one side, as if she didn't understand Belle's question. "I am called . . ." The girl rattled off a string of sounds that Belle couldn't keep up with. She must have noticed Belle's frown, because she added, "You can call me Pin."

Belle introduced Pin to Raider and Melody. Melody's eyes remained red as she continued to scan the orb and Pin. The alien girl didn't seem to mind.

"I am unable to detect any data from her," Melody said.

"Your home helper is a marvelous piece of technology," Pin remarked.

Melody's eyes turned pink, just for a second. The android enjoyed compliments like that. Belle was pleased as well. Too many Martians had been afraid of Melody when they first met her. It was good to find an alien who appreciated Melody for who she was.

"Have you been hiding in that ball all this time?" Belle had to ask.

"Not hiding," Pin said. "Waiting. We were studying your planet and its inhabitants."

That sounded a little frightening to Belle. Maybe her dad was right. And now that Martians had been studied, were these aliens going to be friends or enemies?

Pin turned back to look inside the ball, and a worried expression crossed her face.

"What is it?" Belle asked.

"There is another alien within," Melody answered.

"Yes." Pin frowned. "It is Feyn, my . . . ," she seemed to be searching for a word, ". . . my mother. She is in need of . . . more space. The shuttle is not enough for her . . . condition." Pin spoke deliberately, as if she had to choose every word carefully.

"Oh!" Belle wasn't sure how to respond. What could she do to help two aliens? She didn't know anything about Pin and her people. Was she in danger simply by speaking to her?

Pin stepped closer to Belle and held her hands out to her again.

"Please take my hands," she said. "I can show you all you seek to know."

Belle looked over at Melody. The android had stopped scanning and was simply looking at Pin. Belle hoped that Melody would step in and tell her what to do. But Melody said nothing. Even Raider had stopped whining. He lay between Belle and Pin, looking quite comfortable.

Belle decided that if her closest friends were okay with the alien girl, perhaps there was no danger. She took a step toward Pin and took hold of her hands. Instantly, the world around her seemed to begin spinning faster and faster. But Belle wasn't spinning with it. She was holding onto Pin while Mars whooshed away around them. All Belle felt was a slight breeze.

"Ooh!" Belle cried, squeezing her eyes shut. Her heart was racing.

"There is nothing to worry about," Pin said. Her voice was so calming that Belle felt better.

Belle opened her eyes and looked around. She and Pin were standing in the middle of space, among the stars. Then, as quickly as taking her next breath, Belle was standing on the surface of another planet!

CHAPTER FOUR
:PERGON 3:

"This is my home planet," Pin said, letting go of one of Belle's hands. She held Belle's other hand quite firmly. "We're not really here, but our minds are connected, I am showing you what I remember. Welcome to Pergon 3."

Pergon 3 was the most beautiful place Belle had ever seen. She immediately thought about the stories her grandmother had told her about what Earth was like when she was a child. The sky was a bright blue.

The land was green and brown. A large lake in front of the girls glowed a dark blue-green in the sunlight. It was surrounded by tall, pointy trees. Snow-capped mountains gleamed in the distance.

But here on Pergon 3, there were two objects shining brightly in the sky.

"Ours is a binary system," Pin explained. "We have two suns."

"My friends' ancestors come from a binary system too," Belle said, recalling what she'd learned about Sulux and Nabians.

Pin led Belle through a lovely meadow. Tiny, colorful flowers peeked out of the tall grass, sunning their delicate faces. The air smelled sweet. A calm happiness overcame Belle, and she couldn't help smiling.

"This was my world when I was very young," Pin said. "Our planet was peaceful, and many races from all over the galaxy lived here. Even more came to visit."

"Just like on Mars," remarked Belle.

"That is what we have observed," Pin said, running her hand through the grass.

Belle was surprised that she too could feel the blades gently brush her skin.

"Our star system, Pergonae, has several inhabited planets. Pergon 1 was the seat of government, where all the leaders lived and worked. Pergon 3, my home world, was the holiday planet. My people were famous for being welcoming to all. Our compassionate nature is what made the planet successful."

Pin grew quiet, as if she were thinking of her home. "My last memory of the peaceful time was in this meadow."

"Is the meadow gone now?" Belle asked gently.

Belle recalled how Earth had changed since her grandmother was a child. When Belle had left Earth behind, it was dark and gray, and smelled like smoke on a good day. Thinking about Earth's former beauty made her sad. Had the same thing happened to Pergon 3?

Pin swished her free hand, and the world went spinning again. Now she and Belle were standing in the same meadow, but there were no more flowers or grass. The lake was dried up and the ground was dotted with dead animals. The trees were bare. They looked as burned as the ones around the crater of the Martian crash site. The sky was orange and dark. Large craft hovered over them. The air smelled of rotting food, and Belle heard the distant sound of screaming, crying, and shouting. She looked over to Pin for answers.

"It happened very suddenly," Pin said, sadly. "Pergon 1 elected bad leaders who made bad decisions. The whole system was plunged into despair. Poverty spread quickly, especially on Pergon 2. Many came to Pergon 3 for help. But our resources were used up in a few short years."

Pin led Belle into a small town that looked similar to Sun City. Different aliens milled about, looking sad and hungry. Rough-looking aliens dressed in dark uniforms shoved the sad ones aside, or kicked them as they walked through the streets. Dronelike machines hovered close by, zapping people who got too close to the uniformed aliens.

Belle wanted to run away and hide. But Pin held her steady as they walked through the town.

"People on Pergon 2 soon became restless. They grew tired of being poor and persecuted. Many tried to fight against the authorities," she said. "But to prove their power, the government destroyed Pergon 2. They broadcast it for all to see. The images are burned into my mind forever. I was so scared."

"Is that why your people left your planet?" Belle asked. She couldn't blame them. Their world could be next.

Pin shook her head. "No, we were made to leave. The government on Pergon 1 blamed the problems on the Oirryn Council. They even suggested that we were responsible for the destruction of Pergon 2. We are a very quiet people. We are not good at arguing, even if we are right. So it was easy to blame us.

"Soon, everyone turned against us," Pin continued, "and it became dangerous to even step out of our homes. In their final effort to end the conflict, the government forced all Oirryn to leave. They provided us with ships and sent us away. We have traveled many lightyears to get here. Mars seemed to be the best place to ask for help."

Pin let go of Belle's hand, and the world spun again. Blinking several times, Belle found herself back on Mars in front of the blue ball, with Melody and Raider beside her.

"How long was I gone?" she gasped.

Raider tilted his head and cocked his ears.

"You have been right here, Belle," Melody said. "You have not gone anywhere."

"Wasn't I at least quiet for a long time?" Belle asked. Perhaps only her mind left the planet.

"Your last word was 'Ooh', and you said that exactly four and one half seconds ago," Melody said.

The entire experience had taken less than five seconds!

"It is the easiest way to help others understand our situation," Pin said, looking as if she understood Belle's shock. "To speak it in words would take much longer."

"I agree," Belle said. "If only we were so efficient in our communications."

"What do you want from us?" Melody asked. Her eyes were still in scan mode.

"Please understand that Feyn and I," Pin hesitated, trying to find the right words. "We are not officials. We are ordinary Oirryn. We need help."

"What kind of help?" Belle asked.

"My mother is about to — what is the word — to reproduce?" Pin said.

"Your mom's having a baby?" Belle squealed a little too loudly. She remembered when her mom needed the nurse-android when Thea was born. It was the longest night of Belle's life as she waited outside her parents' bedroom for news of her baby sister.

"Yes," Pin said, looking relieved that someone understood. "But Oirryn require a much larger space than our shuttle here. She cannot stay inside much longer, and I am afraid that these surrounding areas are not safe."

Belle looked around. It definitely wasn't a good place to have a baby.

"How did you turn off the Protectors?" Melody asked.

"I believe we accidentally deactivated them," Pin said. "I don't intend to hurt you, Melody. Will you help us?"

Pin looked and sounded so pitiful that Belle couldn't
help but agree. Of course she had to help. Pin's mom was
having a baby. If Belle and Zara were in Pin's position,
she'd want someone to help them too.

"Please, Melody, we must help," she said.

Without another word, Melody entered the shuttle.

Feyn, Pin's mother, was a delicate-looking woman.
She didn't say a word as Melody lifted her out of the
pod. Her belly was as big as Zara's was when she was
about to have Thea. She had questions for Pin and Feyn,
but this wasn't the time to ask. The Protectors had
begun to whir. They were coming back online. Once
they realized what was happening, they would inform
the authorities, who would then send more Protectors.

"We can hide you in our barn," Belle offered. Melody
didn't disagree, much to Belle's relief. "You'll be safe
there, if you don't mind the smell of turkens."

Belle led them back through the forest. Melody
hovered to give Feyn a smooth ride. The bright
moonlight lit their path back to the farm.

"How did your ball, I mean, shuttle end up here?"
Belle had been dying to know how Pin came to be in her
neighborhood. "Did you research our town?"

Pin stepped carefully over the gravelly road, as if she'd never walked on pebbles before. "No, our ships and the smaller shuttles travel in a tight formation. The shape resembles a twenty-pointed star. Our portion of the formation was hit by some space debris, and our shuttle was caught in Mars' gravity. We were pulled right into your region."

"It's a good thing you landed in an open field, then," Belle said as she opened the farm gate quietly, letting them all through. Pin helped her to shut the gate, and then they ran to catch up with Melody and Feyn.

"I can't tell you how thankful I am," Pin said, as Melody settled Feyn onto a large, soft bed of hay in the warm barn. "I don't know what would've happened if we hadn't met tonight."

Belle promised to bring them some food and water in the morning. As she left her new friends in the upper floor of their barn, Belle had a warm feeling in her heart. She was glad to help.

"Oh dear," Belle said to Melody as they entered their underground house. "I just realized . . . how am I going tell my parents about this?"

Sol 174, Summer/Cycle 106

Almost morning

I was so exhausted that I fell asleep before writing in my journal last night. And then I had the strangest dream. I dreamed that I was Pin and I was on her planet, running with Feyn for our lives. It was so scary, but not because of the war. I felt as if I was Pin! I heard her thoughts, felt her fears, and spoke her words — and I understood them! But I'm sure they weren't in any human language.

It's almost as if . . . no, it can't be. What if when we touched hands, Pin and I became connected in some way? Are we linked somehow? I MUST ask her about that.

Anyway, the dream scared me, and I can't get back to sleep. So, I'm writing instead.

I'm worried about how my parents might react to the aliens in our barn. Maybe I'll wait a while before I tell them. If Feyn has her baby soon, my parents won't have the heart to turn them away. Mom and Dad are softies. They love babies of all species. Hopefully, Feyn won't need a nurse-android to help her have the baby. Will Melody do?

In the meantime, I have to figure out how to get food to them. I wonder what kind of food Oirryn eat?

CHAPTER FIVE
REDVISION NEWS

Sneaking out to the barn with food and water all day was not an easy task. Luckily Melody helped to distract Belle's parents when they wondered why she was checking on Raider so much.

"He had a long night, Zara," Melody said. "He went exploring, and he is exceedingly thirsty now."

Belle hated that she and Melody were lying to her parents. But she needed to be sure they would be on her side before telling them about the strangers in their barn.

"Why are you helping me?" she asked Melody on one of their runs out to the barn. "I know you don't like deceiving my parents, especially if you think it would get me into trouble."

"That is a valid question," Melody said. "And I have a joke about that . . . a human, a Nabian, and an android walked into a restaurant —"

"You're avoiding my question," Belle said. Melody was terrible at keeping secrets. It wasn't in her programming.

"To tell the truth, I cannot explain it," Melody said. "When the aliens first appeared, I went into high alert. But I have been unable to scan either one of them. They have no DNA that I am able to read. I cannot explain it, but when I went into the shuttle to carry Feyn out, a large amount of information about Oirryn history was downloaded into my memory. I am quite determined to help them now."

This worried Belle a bit. Was her own experience with Pin similar to Melody's? Were they being brainwashed into trusting these aliens? Or was the Oirryn's story so sad that they couldn't help but empathize with them? It was hard to tell.

Still, from what Pin had told Belle about Feyn this morning, her big event was coming soon . . . real soon.

Feyn ate everything Belle brought. She said she was so hungry she might start eating the hay.

Each time Belle went to visit, Pin thanked her for helping then.

"You really should stop thanking me," Belle said, feeling bad that she couldn't do more. "I'm sure if the situation were reversed, you would help me."

Pin smiled. "That's true. We Oirryn are known for our compassion and charity."

"It's so odd though, isn't it?" Belle said.

"What is?"

"It's so strange that, all the way across the galaxy, another species looks exactly like us." Belle couldn't help marveling. "Do you suppose we're related in some way?"

Pin's face colored. She looked over at Feyn, who had also gone a bit pink in the cheeks.

"It is a marvel," she said. "Who knows?"

Belle thought about that all the way back to the house. From what she'd seen of Pin's planet, there were a lot of similarities with Earth. Maybe the Oirryn evolved in the same way as humans. She also marveled at the fact that the Oirryn spoke the same language as Belle did. Unless they were so clever that they'd learned it in the few days they were hiding out in the shuttle.

"This is such a muddle." Belle heard Yun's voice as she walked into the house.

"What is?" she asked.

Her parents were watching the news being broadcast over RedVision. A newscaster was reporting on the meetings happening in Utopia between the various Martian authorities and the alien representatives. The newscaster interviewed several people who were attending the meetings.

"They say they need help, but we know so little about them," one Martian said.

"Our records of their system are very limited," said a Nabian representative.

"I am unable to speak freely, because of classified information," said the spokesperson for the Martian government. "But if what we've learned about the Oirryn were to be made public, few Martians would support them living here."

Zara slapped her thighs. "Well, that's comforting!" she exclaimed sarcastically. "If they don't want us to know their secret, why tell us they have one in the first place? That'll just make people more focused on finding out the truth."

"You know politicians," Yun said. "They're always talking in circles."

Belle didn't understand what her dad meant, but she was curious.

"Mom, Dad, what do you think of the aliens?" She sat opposite her parents and tried to read their faces.

"I can't imagine travelling across the galaxy to look for a new home," Zara said. "And when you arrive, people don't even believe your story. It must be frustrating for them."

"That's true!" Belle cried. She took a deep breath, and reminded herself not to get too excited.

"Yet our leaders know more about the aliens than we do," Yun added. "They must have good reasons not to trust them."

Belle frowned. Yun reached over and rubbed the frown lines between her eyes.

"You shouldn't worry yourself over this," he said. "You should head to bed soon. It's getting late. Let the adults handle the difficult decisions."

"It's too early for bed," Belle said. "And I'm done with all my homework."

Belle hated it when her dad treated her like a child. She was fourteen. If only he knew what she'd done to help the Oirryn . . . sometimes he could be so old-fashioned in his thinking.

But after hearing her parents' different opinions, Belle knew she couldn't tell them about Pin and Feyn. Not yet.

The doorbell rang. Belle's heart skipped a beat. Pin wouldn't come looking for her, would she? When Ta'al and Lucas walked in, Belle heaved a sigh of relief.

"Belle, we need to speak to you," Ta'al said quickly as she sped down the stairs. She sounded odd.

When they came into the living room, Belle could see that her friends were wide-eyed and panicky. Yun and Zara, though, didn't seem to notice. They said hello and went right back to watching RedVision.

"What's up?" Belle said, trying to sound normal.

"You need to come with us right now!" Lucas whispered intensely.

Lucas and Ta'al turned right back around and headed up the stairs. They waved for Belle to follow.

Belle shuddered and braced herself. What had her friends discovered?

CHAPTER SIX

:DISCOVERED!:

Belle followed Ta'al and Lucas out to the backyard. Ta'al looked so anxious, her eyes changed color with each breath. Lucas was very pale.

"We were on our way here to see if you wanted to visit the blue ball," Lucas said. As he spoke, he kept his eyes on the barn at the end of the yard. "Local news sites are saying something has changed about the alien object. It sounded exciting, and I thought we could —"

Ta'al huffed and gave Lucas an intense look. He was taking too long to get to the point.

"We think aliens emerged from the ball," Ta'al said, pointing to the barn. "And they're hiding in your barn!"

Belle didn't quite know how to respond. She badly wanted to tell her friends the truth. But she couldn't risk Pin and Feyn being exposed, or worse.

"What makes you think that?" she asked cautiously.

"We saw something," Lucas said. "A beam of light or something shooting out of your barn's roof."

"Lucas yelled in shock," Ta'al said, shooting him a disapproving look. "And the beam disappeared instantly — almost like it was trying to hide from us."

"We have to investigate!" Lucas jumped up and down, trying to contain his excitement, or fear. Or both.

"I think you may have imagined that," Belle said. Even as she spoke she could feel the blood rushing to her face. She turned toward the forest beyond the road, hoping her friends wouldn't notice her reaction. "Why don't we run down to the crash site to see for ourselves?"

Belle headed off to the farm gate.

"Belle!" Ta'al called after her. Belle knew that tone all too well — Ta'al was suspicious. "Why are you in such a hurry to lead us away? That's not like you."

"Yeah," Lucas agreed. "You'd be the first one to check out the barn. Unless . . ."

Ta'al gasped and ran over to confront Belle.

"You know something, don't you?" she demanded. "What are you hiding in there?"

Her friends suddenly bolted toward the barn.

"Wait!" Belle called, but they wouldn't stop.

Belle ran as fast as she could and reached the barn just as Ta'al opened the door.

"Okay, I'll tell you!" Belle cried. "But please wait a minute. I don't want you to scare them."

Lucas and Ta'al froze, staring at Belle.

"Them?" Lucas said. His voice was shaky.

Belle took a deep breath. Then quietly, she explained everything. She told her friends about meeting Pin and Feyn the night before, what she had learned about their people, and how Feyn was expecting a baby.

"I want to see them," Ta'al said, looking up toward the barn's second floor. But of course, nothing could be seen from there. The aliens were well hidden.

"All right," Belle said at last. "But let me go first, to prepare them for visitors."

Ta'al and Lucas stayed several feet behind Belle as she climbed the stairs. Pin was waiting for them at the top.

Behind her was a wall of hay that went all the way around the floor. It resembled a giant nest. Belle guessed that Feyn would be in the middle of that nest.

Pin was happy to meet Belle's friends. Lucas was first to approach her. He waved but said little. She smiled at him and waved back. For just a moment, her skin seemed to turn a light purplish color that matched Lucas' half-Sulux skin. Belle rubbed her eyes. Perhaps the lighting in the barn was playing tricks on her.

When Belle brought Ta'al over to meet Pin, things got even stranger. As Ta'al got closer, Pin began to change. Belle couldn't believe what she was seeing. Pin began to look more and more like a Nabian. Her entire face and body transformed. When Ta'al stood in front of Pin, Belle saw two Nabians, instead of a Nabian and an Oirryn.

"What just happened?" Belle exclaimed. "Why do you look different, Pin?"

"I mentioned that the Oirryn are sensitive to others, did I not?" Pin said, reaching her hands out to Ta'al. "Well, that's because we —"

"You're *pwenthar karaal!*" cried Ta'al.

"*Gyrvel, Nabia sia carnti,*" Pin said, weaving her arms in a traditional Nabian greeting. "Welcome, my Nabian friend."

"She's a shape-shifter," Ta'al said, returning the special greeting.

"What's a shape-shifter?" Belle asked.

Pin turned to Belle, and her appearance changed back to a human-looking girl. Belle took a step back. She clutched Lucas' arm. He was shaking as much as she was.

"I've heard of shape-shifting races," Ta'al said. She wasn't afraid. "I'm honored to meet you."

Pin turned to Ta'al and shifted back into Nabian form. "Oirryn are able to change our shapes to match anyone we meet. We find it makes people more comfortable. We not only look like them, but we can also share their feelings. We take on the joys and pain of those we shift into."

"So what do you really look like?" Lucas blurted out. "Isn't what you're doing kind of like lying?"

Belle thought Lucas had a great point. She began to understand why the people on the news were so nervous about the Oirryn. How could they be trusted if they could disguise themselves as everyone else?

Pin frowned. "I've never thought of it that way. We have always been like this. We would not use our abilities for harm. It is not in our nature." She shifted back to resemble a human girl.

"Did you make yourself look like me just so that I would help you?" Belle's stomach twisted. She didn't like being taken advantage of.

"I thought that looking like you would make it easier to communicate," Pin said. "And I didn't want to frighten you."

"What about your planet then?" Belle asked. "In the vision you showed me, everyone looked human. Even the uniforms and languages were familiar."

"Again, it was done to help you understand our situation, in a way that you could identify with." Pin looked puzzled. "Was I wrong to do so?"

Belle wanted to say that Pin was wrong, that the alien girl should've been honest right from the beginning. But she wasn't sure that was true. If she'd met Pin as a strange-looking alien, she might have been scared, too scared to stop and hear her plea for help. Belle was confused, and she didn't like that feeling.

"Are you really horribly ugly or scary?" Lucas said.

Belle thought that was rude, even if the same questions had popped into her own mind. But Pin didn't seem to mind. She laughed at his question.

"Do you not have a saying? That beauty is in the eye of the beholder?" Pin said.

"Show us what you really look like," Belle said firmly. She couldn't explain why she was annoyed with Pin. She wasn't sure of anything right now.

"You will soon see," Pin said. "My mother will return to her natural form to complete the birth process."

"I don't want to wait," Belle said. She didn't try to hide her anger. She sounded rude, but fear was overcoming her common sense. "I risked a lot to help you. You should at least be honest with me."

Pin pressed her lips tightly together. "That is a reasonable request."

Lucas, Ta'al, and Belle stood back, as if expecting some giant reptilian monster to emerge from Pin's tiny body. They held on to each other for support.

Pin stretched her arms out to her sides and lifted her face to the ceiling. Her feet began to glow with a bright, golden light, similar to the light surrounding the blue ball. The light rose up through her legs, her torso, and finally, her head. She was completely enveloped in golden light. Pin's body was now a glowing figure of light. Belle couldn't make out any features like eyes or a mouth.

"Whoa!" Lucas was the first to speak. "Are you made of solid gold?"

Pin laughed. It was a strange sound — one that reminded Belle of a strong waterfall. It sounded powerful, but it didn't scare her. In fact, she liked it.

"Oirryn are creatures of light and energy," Pin said. Her voice echoed off the barn walls. "While you have solid bodies, we are very different."

"I'll say!" Lucas didn't seem afraid. His face was bright with interest. He took a step closer. "Can I touch you?"

"You may take my hand," Pin said.

"Wait!" Belle warned. "Weird things happen when you touch her."

"Belle is referring to how we communicate," Pin said. "We find it is easier to show you our story, than to tell you with words. It will not hurt."

Pin reached one hand out to Lucas and the other to Ta'al. Belle's best friend had been silent. She seemed doubtful about taking Pin's hand.

"Belle has experienced this already," Pin said. "I didn't hurt her."

Ta'al looked to Belle, who nodded.

"She's right. It was a cool experience," Belle said. "But how do we know you're not brainwashing us?"

Belle heard Pin sigh. It was like the gush of wind when a storm was approaching.

"Belle, you saved our lives, especially my mother's," Pin said. "It would be against everything we believe in to do you harm. This is something our own rulers on Pergon 1 didn't understand. I had hoped that our first connection would overcome the doubts in your heart."

Then Pin lowered her arms. The light dimmed, revealing the human figure Belle had come to know.

"Perhaps this form will make you more comfortable," she said. She reached out her hands again.

"I wouldn't have minded the light version," Lucas said. "Come on, Ta'al, let's give it a try."

Belle was surprised at Lucas. He was the one who was more suspicious at the beginning. But now he was all in. Ta'al must have had the same thought because she stepped forward. Together, Lucas and Ta'al took Pin's hands.

A few seconds later they let go. Their eyes were wide with understanding. Ta'al had tears in her eyes.

"No wonder you helped them," Lucas said, looking back at Belle. "What an incredible journey they've had."

"May we meet Feyn too?" Ta'al asked. Her voice was shaking. She was clearly upset by the Oirryn's troubles.

Pin shook her head. "The full moon will rise soon. Feyn has entered the final phase of reproduction. She is preparing to complete it within the next day."

"She's having the baby tomorrow?" Belle said. "So the light display that Ta'al and Lucas saw will get bigger?"

Pin nodded. "Much bigger. I'm afraid it will attract a lot of attention. But the process cannot be interrupted. We have no choice but to let nature take its course, as you humans say."

Belle was quiet for a long time. She would need to tell her parents as soon as possible. Otherwise, they would discover the aliens in the barn themselves. And everyone, especially Belle, would be in a lot of trouble.

Sol 174, Summer/Cycle 106

Ugh, parents! I tried to tell Mom and Dad about Pin and her mother, but they wouldn't listen. Tonight's news on RedVision revealed the Oirryn's secret. Now everyone knows they're shape-shifters. Mom and Dad were shocked. Some people on the news thought the Oirryn could be invading us, and no one would know how to detect them.

Many people are angry that the authorities let the Oirryn land. I overheard Mom say that all newcomers might be suspected of being Oirryn. She sounded scared. Will people think that we're Oirryn because we're new here too?

CHAPTER SEVEN
:SUSPICIONS:

All day the next day, Belle tried to find the right time to tell her parents about the aliens living in their barn. But all day, her parents were focused on other things.

"RedVision has footage of aliens leaving the blue ball," Yun said at breakfast. "It looks like there were as many as four of them."

Belle almost choked on her food. "Did the cameras get a look at their faces?" she managed to cough out. Her heart was pounding in her throat.

Yun shook his head. "There was too much electrical interference. That's probably what disabled the Protectors there too."

Zara emerged from Thea's room with the baby in her arms. She looked worried. "I just spoke to Myra Walker," she said. "Paddy thinks the aliens could be living amongst us, disguised as regular Martians. She thinks the authorities may begin questioning all recent immigrants."

"Yes, I've been hearing of fights breaking out between neighbors," Yun added. "The idea of shape-shifters amongst us is making people suspicious of each other."

"Mom, are we considered recent immigrants?" Belle wasn't hungry anymore. Her stomach was twisted in a giant knot.

Yun reached over and touched Belle's arm. "Don't worry yourself," he said. "Those were just rumors. We should go about our normal routine and wait to see what the authorities decide."

By the afternoon, Yun had spoken with several different neighbors. Each had their own theory of what would happen next. Only Ta'al's parents brought Belle any comfort.

"We are off to seek the advice of our high council," said So'ark, Ta'al's mother. "He'ern and I will engage our leaders to get more information about the situation. For the Oirryn to travel all this way, and to stay patiently in orbit while negotiations take place, tells me that they are not here to attack us. They cannot help that their nature causes others concern."

"Please let us know what they say," Zara said. "This is all so unsettling."

"Shape-shifting is a tool for survival, for the species who have this ability," He'ern added. "We have not come across many, but the ones we know of are peaceful."

Fa'erz, Ta'al's third parent, nodded from behind, saying nothing. Belle could see Ta'al in the holo-vid too. Her eyes seemed to be begging Belle to tell the truth. But Belle couldn't seem to find the right moment. She was about to finally do it when Melody came into the room with news of her own.

"Talks in the capital have broken down," she reported. "Riots have broken out and Protectors have been called in to control the situation. Negotiations have been suspended and all Oirryn delegates have been detained."

This news upset Yun and Zara so much that they spent the rest of the day in multi-person vid-chat rooms. They discussed the future with the entire neighborhood around Sun City.

Belle had no opportunity to talk to her parents. She snuck in and out all day, bringing food and supplies to her alien friends. No one even noticed her.

That evening, Ta'al, Lucas, and Belle gathered in the barn to talk to Pin.

"We could move you farther away, to an abandoned farm," Belle said. "So you'd be harder to find."

Pin shook her head. She looked tired, as if she hadn't rested at all. "Feyn is too far along in the process to move. It would risk her life as well as the infant's. I'm sorry we've brought on this trouble, but we have no choice now. We have to stay and accept whatever outcome we get."

Belle twisted her fingers together until they hurt. She knew her parents would notice the light show tonight. If the neighbors saw it too, her family would be reported.

"Could Feyn have the baby now?" she asked. At least the remaining sunshine would hide the light show.

"Unfortunately, no," Pin said. "We need the full power of the moon's reflected light."

Melody emerged from behind the nest of hay where Feyn was resting. "From what I have learned, it seems that the process will reach its peak at midnight tonight. Perhaps most people will be asleep by then, and no one will notice."

Ta'al put her hand on Belle's arm. "He'ern and So'ark spoke with our leaders today. They've been working with the council to offer all parties a workable solution. I'm sure they'll have an agreement by tonight."

"Yeah!" Lucas' eyes lit up. "Then everyone will be fine with the Oirryn, and this will be a celebration instead." Belle could tell he was just trying to cheer her up.

The three friends stayed in the barn, in case Feyn needed their help. With every passing minute, the expecting mother's appetite lessened and she looked paler and paler.

The knot in Belle's stomach tightened and grew. She knew her parents could get into serious trouble if the Oirryn were discovered by the authorities. But maybe Melody was right, and all this could happen while the farmers were asleep. The Oirryn baby would be born, and no one would be the wiser for it. She tried to be happy for her new friends, but her imagination kept getting in the way. She thought about how she and Thea would survive without parents. Or how all of them would fare in a prison cell. Or what life would be like if they were sent back to Earth.

"Nothing productive comes from worrying," Melody reminded her.

"What's the news from Utopia?" Belle didn't need to be told to stop worrying. She couldn't help it.

"Talks have been moved to a more secure location," Melody reported. "But there's no news for the public yet."

Night came too quickly. Before Belle knew it, her parents were insisting she prepare for bed.

"Dad, what will happen when those aliens are found?" she asked after dinner.

"It depends on how the talks go in Utopia," he said.

"If someone shelters them, will the authorities send them back to their home planet? Or put them in prison?"

Zara took the dishes out of Belle's hands. She placed them in the washer, and turned to Belle. "All right, young lady," she said. "Something is up. What are you hiding?"

Belle blinked several times. She felt like crying but that would give everything away. "Nothing," she said. "I'm just . . . curious, that's all."

But her parents wouldn't believe her. They watched and waited until Belle couldn't stand it any longer.

She burst into tears.

"I'm so sorry," she blubbered. "I didn't know what else to do. I tried to tell you before, but you . . . you . . . wouldn't listen."

Zara helped Belle to a chair. "It's okay Belle. Just start from the beginning," she said. "Tell us everything."

The words tumbled out of Belle as she recounted the story of how she found Pin and Feyn. By the time she was done, her parents' faces were pale, and they didn't say anything for ages.

"And that's happening tonight?" Yun said at last.

Belle nodded. "Please, we have to help them. The baby will die if they get taken away tonight."

Yun and Zara insisted on meeting the aliens in the barn. They agreed to hold off on informing the authorities until after speaking with Pin.

Meeting the Oirryn was as shocking for Belle's parents as it had been for her friends. Neither Yun nor Zara would take Pin's hands, though, so Belle resorted to telling them what she'd experienced.

Just as Belle finished her story, Feyn let out a loud cry. As she did, the entire barn lit up with light. Zara grabbed Belle, wrapping her arms around her daughter.

"It's all right, Mom," Belle said. "Feyn is just getting closer to having her baby."

At Feyn's next cry, a beam of light shot upwards to the ceiling, burning a small hole in the roof. The Songs ran outside to see that the narrow beam of light pierced the darkening sky, reaching up toward the full moon.

"Oh no!" Zara gasped. "Everyone will see it."

"I'm so sorry, Mom," Belle said.

"No," Zara said. "Don't be. You were just being you, Belle. You are always helping those in need. You should never be sorry for that."

"But, what about the authorities?" Belle cried.

Yun put his arm around Belle. "Let us worry about that. We should do whatever we can to help Feyn now. There's no going back."

Belle couldn't believe how amazing her parents were being. If she was a helpful person, it was because she had learned it from her mom and dad. This was what she'd hoped for. If only there wasn't so much trouble to face for their kindness.

For the next few hours, the Songs and Melody did what they could to help. They did everything they could to make Feyn comfortable. Yun and Zara listened with curiosity while Pin told them stories of her home planet.

As the night went on, the hole in the roof grew wider as each beam of light grew stronger and bigger. Belle knew the light would likely attract attention. Before long, the sound of approaching hover-wagons confirmed her fears.

CHAPTER EIGHT
:AN ANGRY MOB:

Several hover-wagons rumbled through the Songs' farm gate just before midnight. They formed a semi-circle, blocking the path to and from the house. Locked in the stables, Raider barked at the sound of their approach.

One by one, the Songs' neighbors emerged from their transports carrying blasters or makeshift weapons. The Walkers, the Senns, and several other neighbors stood in front of their wagons. They advanced toward the Songs as one, as if they hadn't all been great friends for the last year.

"We saw the light beam in the sky," Mrs. Senn said. "We followed it here."

"Are you all okay?" said Mr. Senn. "Are those aliens in your barn?"

"Yes, they are. But let us explain," said Zara.

"*What?* I can't believe you're harboring the fugitives!" Paddy exclaimed. "Why did you lie to us?"

Yun held out his hands, as if to hold them back. "You need to listen first," he said.

"Are you one of them?" Mr. Senn said.

"Don't be ridiculous," Zara jumped in.

"We're just giving them temporary shelter," Yun explained, raising his voice so all could hear. "They need our help."

"When it's all over, we'll turn them over to the authorities," Zara said.

"When what's all over?" Myra stepped forward. "What is this light show? Some kind of weapon?"

Lucas and Ta'al burst through the crowd to stand next to Belle.

"The alien is having a baby," Lucas shouted. "And we have to protect them so the new life doesn't get hurt."

"The light is a part of the process for them," Belle said. "They're creatures of light."

Whispers of astonishment spread through the crowd. But their faces didn't show fascination, as Belle had hoped. They showed fear.

"Come over here with us," Myra hissed at Lucas. "You don't know what you're getting yourself into."

"No," Lucas said defiantly. "They're our friends, and we're going to help them."

"That's right," Ta'al said. "They're peaceful people. They don't mean us any harm."

Belle couldn't have been prouder of her friends.

"They've been brainwashed!" someone cried out.

Yun stepped forward. "Now, hold on. Let's all just calm down and talk this out."

Belle stepped forward to join her dad. "At exactly midnight, Feyn will have her baby. There will be a bright beam of light. They need the energy from the moonlight to complete the birth process. If everyone could be patient, you'll see that they're friendly. They're just refugees, in need of our help."

Belle looked at each of her neighbors with pleading eyes. "Just over a week ago, you were all here at my birthday party. When we first moved here, we were strangers too. You didn't know us. We could've been horrible people. But you welcomed us, and we've become good friends."

She pointed to the barn with tears in her eyes. "It's the same situation here. The Oirryn need us to trust them. If we don't, then who will? Let's help Feyn have her baby. You'll see that they're good people."

Yun took Belle's hand in his, and gave it a squeeze. "No matter the outcome tonight," he said, "I'm so proud of you."

Zara walked up to Belle and smiled at her too. Thea clapped and giggled. Lucas and Ta'al squeezed in between Belle's parents and each took her hand.

The night air was still and quiet. For the longest time, no one said anything. Suddenly a wide beam of light shot out of the barn roof and into the sky. It was as if someone was painting the night sky with a fat brush. The beam broke apart into horizontal waves of color — blue, green, pink, and yellow. It looked like a wavy, sideways rainbow.

The crowd gasped. One person fainted.

Belle felt happy and peaceful all at once. She could feel a silly smile crossing her face. She looked over at her friends. They had the same silly smile too. Were they all experiencing Pin's emotions?

Belle looked over at her parents. The beauty of the light show mesmerized them. Thea was enjoying the display too. The horizontal colors twisted and grew bigger over the next few moments. Then the silence of the night was shattered by a piercing cry. It sounded like a combination of a clap of thunder, a scream, and an explosion. There were no Martian words to describe it. Belle knew it was Feyn, but the others didn't.

"I knew it was a weapon!" one neighbor shouted.

"They've brainwashed all of you!" another said.

Several farmers moved forward, closer to the Songs.

"No!" Belle cried, stepping back toward the barn door. Lucas and Ta'al went with her.

"Stay back!" insisted Yun. "This is our property and you have no right to behave like this."

"Get out of our way, Yun," Paddy said. "We have to make sure they're not going to harm us."

"I assure you, they're not." Belle was yelling over the crowd now. But no one was listening. Feyn's cry had scared them too much.

"Lucas, you come over here," Paddy Walker demanded.

"No, Dad," Lucas said. "They're not dangerous!"

"You kids should not have gotten involved," Paddy said. "Yun and Zara, I'm disappointed in you."

"My parents didn't know about the aliens until today," Belle said. She didn't like that her parents were being blamed for what she did.

"Dad, we chose to help them on our own," Lucas added.

"You have no idea how dangerous these aliens are!" shouted Mr. Senn, shaking his fist at Belle. "Someone call the Protectors!"

"No, wait!" Belle yelled. Her heart was pounding so hard it hurt. She felt great fear and knew that these were Pin's feelings more than her own. She could feel Pin begging for a little more time.

Suddenly another cry and another shot of light burst into the air. The neighbors fell back again. Several cried out in fear. The sky lit up in the most amazing light show of the night. Ribbons of color floated across their view. The stars even seemed to shine more brightly. The moon glowed silver and gold and loomed extra-large over the barn. It was the most beautiful sight Belle had ever seen.

Everyone was entranced. For a moment, they'd all forgotten their fear and anger. For several minutes, everyone felt happy. Belle felt as if Pin's feelings were spreading through the whole crowd. The Oirryn baby had arrived, and with it, there was joy and happiness.

Unfortunately, that joy lasted only a few seconds. As if coming out of a trance, one by one, the neighbors grew angry again. And afraid. They demanded that Belle, Ta'al, and Lucas move away.

They were ready to storm the barn.

CHAPTER NINE
:A NEW LIFE:

Belle pressed her back against the heavy barn door. Lucas and Ta'al gripped the door handles. The angry farmers moved in closer. Belle felt like she was about to be swallowed by an enormous monster. She squeezed her eyes shut and prepared for the worst.

"Stop! Don't be ridiculous." Zara moved in front of them. "You're adults. You should be ashamed of yourselves. Isn't this what we hope for our children, to stand up for what they believe in? Let's give them a chance."

Yun took his place in front of his family and they all faced the anxious crowd together.

Belle breathed a huge sigh of relief. She knew she could count on her parents to be on her side, no matter how much trouble she caused.

"Please," Belle said. "Let me tell you their story."

"Let her speak!" Yun shouted over the crowd's objections.

Before Belle could say a word, the barn door opened behind them. Melody stepped out first, followed by Pin.

Or at least, it looked like Pin, but older. It was an adult version of Pin.

She stepped into the open. Belle realized that Pin had to appear as an adult to get the neighbors to listen to her. Pin could also understand the Martians' fears as she tried to protect her mother and the new baby.

Melody raised her hands to the crowd. "What you have witnessed in the light display is a reaction with Mars' electromagnetic field. During the birth process, the Oirryn produce a chemical that causes the air to light up in colors. There is nothing to be alarmed about."

"How can we be sure it's harmless?" Paddy asked. He looked both scared and bewildered. "Are there any side effects?"

"I can show you the details of the process, if you wish," Melody offered. A panel in her torso lit up with all kinds of charts and figures. Paddy squinted at it and shrugged.

Pin glanced at the android and nodded. She stretched out her hands toward the neighbors. "If you take my hands, I can explain this much more quickly."

Every farmer took a step back at the same time.

"All right," Pin said, lowering her hands. "In words that you will understand, I wish to announce that Feyn, my mother, has just had a baby. Our people are not able to change our shape until we mature. So the new life in the barn behind me remains in our true form."

"Do not be afraid," Melody added. "It is a beautiful sight, even to an android like myself."

"Would you like to see our new addition?" Pin offered.

The neighbors were too busy staring at Pin and the lingering light show above the barn to answer right away.

"Showing us your baby won't change the fact that we don't really trust you," Myra said. Her words broke the hypnotic feeling in the air.

"Would you trust us more if your government chose to accept us?" Pin asked.

The farmers murmured among themselves.

"I guess so," Paddy said reluctantly. "But just a little."

"When we're in our natural state, our thoughts are connected," Pin explained. "That's how I know about our leaders' decisions. As of this hour, the Martian authorities have reached an arrangement with my people. I believe that one of your own neighbors has played a part in achieving this deal." Pin looked over at Ta'al.

Ta'al's eyes reflected the many colors in the sky. "My parents helped during the negotiations."

"Surely this is a positive sign?" Pin said. "Your people are beginning to trust us."

"I haven't heard that news," Paddy said.

Melody's eyes turned blue as she accessed the news. "I can confirm that Pin is correct. The Utopian governing authority has just announced that a deal has been reached to provide space for the Oirryn to live on Mars."

Several neighbors consulted their communication devices and confirmed the news. This calmed the people a little, although Belle still heard some mumbling. The neighbors were not completely convinced.

"Mr. Walker, would you take Pin's hand?" Belle asked. She knew that if Lucas' dad understood the Oirryn's ordeal, he could convince the rest of their neighbors. "Lucas, Ta'al, and I have learned so much by taking this step in trusting Pin."

"Please, Dad?" Lucas said. He took his dad's hand, as Pin extended hers.

Paddy Walker looked unsure at first. But after looking at his son, then back at his wife, he took Pin's hand. Five seconds later, he broke the connection.

"Myra, you need to do this," he said somberly. Then, turning to the rest of the neighbors, he tried his best to explain what he had learned.

"I know this situation is strange, but I think we should give the Oirryn a chance," he said. "They've suffered a great deal, and Pin's story seems true to me. I can't really explain it, I just feel it."

Myra released Pin's hand and wiped a tear away from her face. "I agree. These people need our help."

The mood amongst the farmers grew more positive. Not everyone was willing to take Pin's hand, but those that did told the others of their experience. Slowly, the neighbors laid down their weapons. Some still kept their distance, but they were no longer hostile.

"Could we see the new baby Oirryn?" Belle asked. She'd been dying to know what it looked like.

Pin raised her hands over her head. Everyone looked up. Through the ribbons of light, a bright, golden figure floated out of the barn roof and down into Pin's arms.

Pin cradled the glowing alien baby. It was about a fourth of the size of an adult Oirryn. Belle couldn't make out any features — it just looked like a blob of light to her.

A few people gasped at the sight of a flying baby alien, but they didn't say anything negative. Thea giggled in delight, clapping her hands at the sight.

"Is it a boy or a girl?" Zara asked.

"The Oirryn can take either form," Pin said. "But our kind have no need for a specific gender."

"That's similar to Nabians," Ta'al said. "We have more genders than humans do, and it is hard to explain it to them. We have to simplify our concepts to fit their understanding."

Belle never knew that Ta'al felt that way. She decided that she needed to try harder to learn more about her best friend's people.

As Pin held her new sibling, the neighbors approached, one by one. They asked a lot of questions, and Pin did her best to answer them. Belle was glad that no one was shouting anymore.

In that moment of quiet, Belle heard an all too familiar sound — the whirring of engines in the air — drones!

"Who called the Protectors?" Yun asked, looking up as the drones headed toward the crowd.

No one would admit to reporting the Oirryn. A bolt of fear shot through Belle's body. She knew Pin was afraid, even though she didn't show it on her face.

"Please, we need the night to rest," Pin said. Her voice rose over the hum of the drones' engines. "The baby is still weak. We will leave in the morning, and you will have no trouble from us."

"We can't let the Protectors take them," Belle cried. With every passing second, she felt Pin's panic grow. Some of her own fear was mixed in too. It made Belle very uncomfortable.

Out of the darkness, a row of Protectors appeared. Their red eyes glowed like warning beacons. Together, they stomped their way toward the Songs' barn. Melody stepped in to remind them of the agreement that had been reached in Utopia.

"That does not apply here. These are fugitives," the lead Protector said in a flat voice. "We have orders to bring them in immediately."

"Quick, get back inside!" Belle cried, practically shoving Pin and the baby through the barn door. "We'll hold them off as long as possible."

"We'll go with you," Zara said, carrying Thea. Zara pulled the barn door shut with a thud.

Yun stood guard outside the barn next to his daughter. He picked up an ultra-sonic blaster and held it against his chest, a warning to all who might try and pass. Paddy and Myra took their place next to Yun. A few other neighbors stepped up too. Others murmured in fear, and ducked behind the line of oncoming Protectors, choosing not to be a part of the confrontation.

Melody, Lucas, and Ta'al moved to stand with Belle. Together, they formed a wall against the giant Protectors.

The Protectors edged in closer. There was a moment of tense silence. Belle squealed softly. She had no idea how this situation would be resolved. They'd prevented a stampede of farmers. Would they now be trampled by the giant androids instead? Would Pin, Feyn, and the new baby be taken away to suffer a fate Belle could not imagine?

The line of Protectors took another step closer. The cloud of drones above descended. Belle's squeal grew louder. Her heart was pounding so hard it felt like it might jump right out of her chest.

How would this night end?

CHAPTER TEN

⋮CONFRONTATION⋮

The beautiful waves of color in the night sky vanished under the harsh white lights shining from each drone. The buzzing machines surrounded the barn, combing every surface of the building for an opening. Belle knew that if they found even the slightest crack, they would swoop inside and capture her new friends.

She could not — would not — allow that.

The line of Protectors advanced another step. The neighbors behind them followed closely behind.

"Let them do their job!" a voice called out from behind the line of huge silver and black androids. Belle was shocked at how quickly her neighbors had changed their minds. Only a moment ago, they had begun to accept the Oirryn. Now, they were ready to give them up.

"You are to stand down," the lead Protector said, stepping closer. "We must remove the aliens from this building. It is the law."

"We won't move!" Belle yelled back. "Leave us alone!"

"Belle, the Protectors can't make their own decisions," Yun said, nudging his daughter. "They have orders."

Belle turned to her oldest friend. "Melody," she whispered. "Can you do something?"

"I have an idea." Melody engaged her anti-gravity function and hovered off the ground.

"Do what you can," Belle said. "We need to give the Oirryn as much time as possible."

Melody floated over to meet the lead Protector.

"I'd better try to help," Paddy Walker volunteered, following Melody.

"I don't like this. We should do what they say," Myra Walker said, wrapping her arm around Lucas. Belle knew she was worried for his safety. Lucas had been kidnapped once, and Myra was not going to let him be harmed again.

"No way, I'm not moving," Lucas said, sounding very determined. His mother sighed.

Suddenly a drone hovering above the barn roof widened its beam of light.

"Surrender yourselves and no harm will come to you," a loud voice boomed from its speaker.

Belle craned her neck to see that the drone had found the hole in the roof that was made during the baby's birth.

"No!" cried Belle. She started to open the barn door.

"Don't do that," Yun said. "The Protectors may charge."

Belle could feel her hands and legs shaking. She knew that inside the barn, Pin was terrified. Belle shut her eyes and took a deep breath. A strange calm overcame her and she closed her eyes. In her mind, she pictured herself standing right by Pin in the upper level of the barn. How was this happening?

Belle, I'm so glad you found our connection, Pin said. The alien was in her child form again. Her thoughts were filling Belle's mind. *I've been trying to reach you.*

So we are connected! Belle wasn't sure if she was scared or excited. All her emotions were jumbled up in this moment.

We will always be, Pin replied. *You were the first of your kind to touch me, and that moment sealed our connection. My link to the others is weaker. But ours will always be strong.*

Belle felt sad. It felt as if Pin was saying goodbye to her.

You have to do something, Belle told Pin. *You can't let them take you.*

There is little that we can do, Pin responded. *Feyn and the little one need to rest. They are in danger of losing their lives if they do not.*

They'll die? Belle couldn't bear to think she could be responsible for hurting her new friends.

Suddenly Feyn shifted into her natural, light form. Beams of her natural light burst through the small hole in the roof, just as when the baby was born.

Belle heard shouts all around her. The drones' engines also grew louder.

She opened her eyes. For a second, the drones hovering over the roof zoomed backward to avoid Feyn's light beams. The lead Protector stopped talking to Paddy and Melody and ordered the others to line up in a defensive position.

The neighbors standing with Belle and her friends fled.

"They're going to charge the barn!" Myra cried.

"I won't let them hurt my friends," Lucas shouted, as his mom pulled him away from the door.

The lead Protector swiped his arm at Melody. Luckily, she was hovering, so she only flew backward a few meters. The Protector marched toward the barn door and the others followed their leader. Yun stepped forward, and Paddy ran at them from behind. The giant androids pushed them both aside.

"Dad!" Belle cried, as she watched her father lose his balance and fall on his back.

"I'm fine!" Yun called out. "Get out of the way, Belle!"

Belle ducked between two Protectors as they walked by. The first Protector smashed his hand through the barn door and pulled it off its hinges. Startled turkens screeched in fear. In the distance, Raider's bark was fierce.

Belle tried to follow the Protectors into the barn, but they kept pushing her farther and farther back. All the neighbors rushed in after the Protectors. Belle couldn't see her Dad or Paddy, or any of her friends. She was jostled by panicked bodies, and even elbowed in the face.

She pulled back for a moment to find her balance and rub her sore nose. Looking up at the barn roof, she saw the golden light beam from Feyn meet the harsh white light from a drone. There was a short burst, as if the lights meeting caused an explosion of some kind.

Without thinking, Belle dashed around to the side of the building and climbed the ladder that led to the roof. She didn't know what she was doing, but she knew she had to do something to save Pin and Feyn.

"You leave my friends alone!" She yelled over and over, as she climbed.

When she reached the roof, she crawled on all fours because of the steep slope. She reached the hole in the roof just as more sparks were firing between the light beams. A spark landed on the back of her neck and burned her skin. She cried out but kept going. She couldn't let a little pain stop her from saving her friends.

When she reached the hole in the roof, she turned to face the drone and sat down. She used her body to break the connection between the two light beams, and to keep the drone from entering through the barn roof.

"Remove yourself from the scene," a voice ordered through the drone's speaker.

It retracted its light beam, and all Belle could see was a dark shape hovering in the sky.

"Make me!" She couldn't tell where the anger and feirceness were coming from. Was it hers, or Pin's, or a combination of both?

To Belle, the whole world stopped for several long minutes. She glared at the drone that was determined to get past her. Belle focused on her breathing. It seemed to be the loudest sound at the moment. It even drowned out the hum of the drone's engine.

"You have been warned," the drone's operator said through its speaker.

Belle's heart skipped a beat. In that instant, the drone flew over her. Then it opened a compartment and shot something at her. Before she could move, her shoulders and arms were covered in a sticky net.

Belle screamed. The drone lifted off, carrying her higher into the sky. Half her body was trapped in the net, while the other half dangled dangerously beneath the drone. Belle kicked and wriggled as the drone flew past the barn roof. She twisted hard and one arm came loose.

She screamed again. With only one arm in the drone's net, Belle was in a perilous position. She looked down. People were looking up at her. Some were pointing, others had their hands clapped over their mouths. Belle saw her dad. He was yelling at a Protector to do something.

Melody hovered up to Belle and the drone.

"Help me," Belle begged her android.

Melody held her arms as if to steady Belle.

"Do not wiggle so much," she warned. "The net is meant to cover your whole body. That is how drones carry their prisoners. Somehow it only caught a part of you."

"I know that!" Belle couldn't help feeling annoyed and scared at the same time. "Please, just help me get down."

Melody looked directly at the drone. "You do not want to be responsible for hurting a member of our own community." Hopefully, its operator was a reasonable person.

The drone jerked to the left. A tiny part of the sticky net gave way. Belle shrieked.

The drone moved back toward the barn roof. At least now if Belle fell, she'd land on the roof. The thought didn't give her much comfort. But it was better than falling all the way to the hard ground below.

Melody matched the drone's movements again. Her arms were stretched toward Belle, ready to catch her.

"Do not move," Melody warned again.

"I'm trying," Belle said. She could feel tears welling up behind her eyes.

"Look at me," Melody said.

Belle did. Melody's eyes were purple. They'd never been purple before. Belle didn't know what function that was for.

"Just keep your eyes on me," Melody repeated.

This was most puzzling to Belle.

Melody began to count. "One . . . Two . . ."

"What are you doing?" Belle asked.

But before Melody finished, several things happened.

A blaster shot hit the drone from below. It had no effect. Drones were protected from blasts like that. But it made the drone turn to look at who had shot at it.

It was Yun.

Then, while the drone was distracted, something attacked it from behind! Something with wings and claws and a giant beak! The creature pierced the drone's tough hull with its beak, causing it to veer to the side and release the net.

Belle fell. But just before she hit the roof, giant claws clamped themselves around her shoulders. She felt herself soaring as the mystery creature shot into the air. Before Belle could even catch a breath to scream, she looked up.

Above her was a magnificent bird that she'd never seen before. It had golden feathers and had huge wings that acted like a wide parachute. As it descended to the ground, it lowered its head to look at Belle. The bird had her new friend's eyes. It was Pin! Her alien friend had shape-shifted into this bird creature to save her life.

Pin lowered Belle gently to the ground. Her parents came running to her, followed by her friends and neighbors. People applauded.

"That was amazing!" Paddy Walker exclaimed. "You Oirryn are something else."

Pin returned to the form of a girl. "I'm just glad that Belle is unhurt."

All the neighbors surrounded Belle and Pin. They praised the Oirryn girl for her bravery and kindness.

"I told you they were good," Belle said. She was still shaking from the fright. "All they ask is for one peaceful night to rest."

Murmurs of agreement spread through the crowd. Zara and Yun hugged their daughter. Thea gave her a big squeeze around her neck.

A minute later, Melody appeared around the corner of the barn. "I have come to an agreement with the Protectors," she said. "They have the Secretary of Utopia on their comm links. They wish to speak to someone about this situation."

"I'll speak to them," Yun said. He gave Belle another hug. "Just don't get into any more trouble while I'm negotiating, okay?"

Belle nodded. "I've had enough excitement for one day," she said.

"For a lifetime," Ta'al corrected.

Yun and Paddy spoke to the authorities for a long time. When they were done, they came back to the crowd.

"In light of the recent agreement in Utopia, the Secretary has ordered the Protectors and drones to stand down," Yun said. Belle breathed a sigh of relief.

"But it's only for one night," Paddy added. "Tomorrow, the aliens . . . er, I mean, the Oirryn, will have to surrender themselves to the authorities."

"No!" Belle couldn't believe she'd still lost.

"It's okay, Belle," Pin said quietly. "It is necessary, so that there may be peace between our people and Mars."

"She's right," Yun said. "The Secretary assured me that the Oirryn will be treated with respect. They are all eager to find a happy solution for their situation."

"At least they'll have tonight to rest," Zara added. "Feyn certainly needs it."

But Belle was still worried.

"Fine," she said loudly to all who were listening. "Pin and Feyn and the new baby will rest tonight in our barn. And I'm going to camp out here to keep them safe."

"As will I," Ta'al added with a smile. "I love having a *matekap* — sleepover!"

"Count me in too," Lucas said.

Paddy patted Yun on the back. "Looks like it's a family camping night." He laughed.

"I will fetch the tents and equipment," said Melody.

Sol 176, Summer/Cycle 106

Pin decided to join Lucas, Ta'al, and me in our tent. We stayed up really late to talk. Feyn and the baby are safe and resting in the barn. Melody has agreed to watch over them for the night. She's really taken a liking to the Oirryn.

Pin told us stories about her home planet, and her life from before they left. She even showed us her memories again when we all held hands. It turns out Pin is about a hundred cycles old. For the Oirryn, that's still young. They live for hundreds of cycles! Wouldn't it be amazing to live that long?

Lucas and Ta'al have fallen asleep. As I write, Pin is rubbing Raider's ears. He likes her too. She seems to be communicating with him. I've never seen him so happy.

I'm really tired too, but I don't want to sleep. After tomorrow, I may never see my friend again. We're still connected in a strange way, and Pin says it will always be like that. We'll be able to "talk" to each other through our connection, no matter how far away she goes. It's kind of strange, but I'm glad that we'll always be together in a way.

But I'm still sad that she has to leave.

CHAPTER ELEVEN
:THE BEST WE:
COULD DO

Belle clutched Thea's tiny hands to help her pull herself up to a sitting position. Her head bobbled a little, but she had a huge grin on her face. Raider lay behind her as if he was trying to keep her from falling backward.

"She'll be standing and walking in no time at all," Zara said, adjusting a fence pole that one of the alpacas had knocked down.

Belle didn't say much. Her mind wasn't on her baby sister or the curious alpaca nibbling at her mom's

shoulder. It had been a week since Pin, Feyn, and the new
Oirryn baby had been taken away by the Protectors. The
Secretary who had spoken to Yun had been nice enough
to wait until the Oirryn were ready to be moved. By
noon the next day, they'd escorted the aliens away. Ta'al's
parents went with them too. So'ark wanted to make sure
the Oirryn would be treated well and kept safe. Pin's last
words to Belle were a promise to keep in touch.

But there had been very little news about her and her
family since. The silence troubled Belle. With each passing
day, the sinking feeling in her stomach got worse.

"Belle?" Zara's voice broke through Belle's thoughts.
"Were you even listening to me?"

"I'm sorry, Mom," Belle said. "I was daydreaming."

Zara sighed. "I understand that you're worried," she
said. "But I think you should go and see what Dad wants.
He's been calling for you."

Sure enough, when Belle looked over at their house,
she saw Yun waving at her.

"I have news!" he cried.

Belle scooped Thea up and walked as fast as she could
to her dad. News! She'd been waiting for that all week.
As she got closer, Yun went inside the house. When she
reached the door, Raider followed her inside.

"Down here," Yun said, waving at her to follow. "There's someone who'd like to say hello."

Could Pin actually be here in her house?

Belle sighed in disappointment when she saw that it was just a holo-vid communication. On the dining table was a holographic projection of her Oirryn friend. Pin wasn't really here, but it was better than nothing.

"Pin would like a word with you," Yun said, heading back up the stairs.

"How are you, Pin?" Belle asked, as she placed Thea in her playpen. "Do you have a new home? Is it far away? How's the baby? And Feyn?"

Pin laughed, raising her hands. "You ask so many questions. I don't know where to begin."

"Sorry," Belle said, trying to calm herself. She sat in front of the holo-vid, and took two deep breaths. "Let's start again. Are you well?"

Pin nodded. "We are all well," she said. "The talks with the Martian authorities have gone well. All Oirryn who have children or need medical attention have been allowed to land on the planet. That is a good start."

"But where are you staying?" Belle asked.

"For now, we are in a camp near Utopia," Pin said. "But very soon, we will be moving to some land near you."

Belle bounced in her seat. "That's wonderful news!" Baby Thea, who seemed to be listening, gurgled and bounced in her pen. "Where, exactly?"

Pin pulled up a holo-map behind her. She pointed at a region in Olympia just beyond Sun City.

"The Barren Lands?" Belle was surprised. There was nothing out there. Terraforming had never been completed in that area. It was nothing but red sand and rocks. There were no houses, or plants, or roadways out there. The only major location was the Nabian-Sulux archaeological site that she and Ta'al had discovered earlier that summer.

Pin seemed to read all those thoughts in Belle's face. "We Oirryn adapt easily to whatever environment we're in. And the authorities have agreed to do some terraforming to help us be more comfortable."

"But it looks nothing like your old planet," Belle said, feeling disappointed.

"We were not expecting to find that," she said. "Only a livable space, where we may exist in peace. This is more than we had hoped for."

Belle wasn't so sure of that. But she was glad that her friend was safe. She chatted for a while longer, until Thea started to fuss. It was almost time for her lunch.

"I hope you can visit us some time," Pin said. "Or I could come to you."

"Yes!" Belle was excited to hear that. "I would love to see you again. There's so much we can do, places we can go to explore —"

"One thing at a time," Pin said, holding up her hand with a laugh. "I must go now. We're making preparations to move. Give our greetings to your parents and Melody."

"I hope you like your new home," Belle said. "We'll see each other soon."

Pin waved to Thea as her image fizzled out.

"It was nice for her to send her greetings to me," Melody said, walking into the room with Thea's lunch. "It has been a unique experience, meeting the Oirryn. It makes me wonder about the many species of aliens that we have yet to meet."

"I didn't know androids could wonder about things like that," Belle said.

"I am learning to be curious," Melody said. "It is a very human trait."

Belle sat Thea in her feeding chair, and Melody helped as the baby tried to feed herself. Belle felt better now that she knew Pin was safe, and even a little excited that they would see each other again soon.

As Thea gurgled and swallowed her food, Belle's mind drifted again. She dreamed of the adventures she would soon have with Ta'al, Lucas, and her newest friend, Pin.

Sol 4, Autumn/Cycle 106

Pin said that Feyn and the baby were doing well. In fact, the baby is bigger than Thea, and is "mobile". That's the word Pin used. I think she meant the baby is walking around already. I guess Oirryn children develop fast.

I'm glad they have a new home. Melody and I did some research on the new terraforming work being done in the Barren Lands. It looks like they're making good progress. And several buildings have been put up already, so maybe it won't be so bad. It'll probably be a whole new town, just for the Oirryn. I wonder what they'll name it?

I'm just happy that Pin will be near enough for us to visit. Even though she's much older, she's a lot of fun. I wonder what kind of adventures we can have together? After all, she can fly!

ABOUT THE AUTHOR

A.L. Collins learned a lot about writing from her teachers at Hamline University in St. Paul, MN. She has always loved reading science fiction stories about other worlds and strange aliens. She enjoys creating and writing about new worlds, as well as envisioning what the future might look like. Since writing the Redworld series, she has collected a map of Mars that hangs in her living room and a rotating model of the red planet, which sits on her desk. When not writing, Collins enjoys spending her spare time reading and playing board games with her family. She lives near Seattle, Washington with her husband and five dogs.

• • • ● ● ● • •

ABOUT THE ILLUSTRATOR

Tomislav Tikulin was born in Zagreb, Croatia. Tikulin has extensive experience creating digital artwork for book covers, posters, DVD jackets, and production illustrations. Tomislav especially enjoys illustrating tales of science fiction, fantasy, and scary stories. His work has also appeared in magazines such as *Fantasy & Science Fiction, Asimov's Science Fiction, Orson Scott Card's Intergalactic Medicine Show,* and *Analog Science Fiction & Fact.* Tomislav is also proud to say that his artwork has graced the covers of many books including Larry Niven's *The Ringworld Engineers,* Arthur C. Clarke's *Rendezvous With Rama,* and Ray Bradbury's *Dandelion Wine* (50th anniversary edition).

:WHAT DO YOU THINK?:

1. In this story, Belle was determined to help the Oirryn, even though others were suspicious of them. Why do you think Belle reacted differently?

2. Why do you think the Martian people were afraid when they saw the Oirryn? Would you be afraid too? Why or why not?

3. Several groups of refugees on Earth today are looking for new homes. Find out about a group of refugees and what life is like for them. Are their experiences similar to what the Oirryn had to endure in the story?

4. Write a story from the point of view of an Oirryn refugee. Describe what the alien's journey to Mars was like. How would they feel about having to settle on a new planet that is so different from their home world?

5. Imagine that you were a shape-shifting alien like the Oirryn. Write a story about an adventure you could have as a shape-shifter.

:GLOSSARY:

asylum (uh-SYE-luhm) — protection given to people escaping from danger in their own land

hazmat suit (HAZ-mat SOOT) — a special suit that protects a person's entire body from hazardous materials, such as toxic chemicals and radiation

idealistic (ahy-dee-uh-LIS-tik) — having a strong sense of what is right or how things should be

investigate (in-VESS-tuh-gate) — to gather facts in order to learn as much as possible about something

meteor (MEE-tee-ur) — a piece of rock that burns up as it passes through the atmosphere

poverty (PAW-vuhr-tee) — the state of being poor or without money

radiation (ray-dee-AY-shuhn) — tiny particles sent out from radioactive material

refugee (ref-yuh-JEE) — a person who is forced to flee a place to escape war or natural disasters

superstition (soo-pur-STIH-shuhn) — a belief that an action can affect the outcome of an event

terraform (TER-uh-form) — to change the environment of a planet or moon to make it capable of supporting life

torso (TOR-soh) — the part of the body between the neck and waist, not including the arms

:MARS TERMS:

holo-vid (HOHL-uh-vid) — a holographic projection that shows videos for information or entertainment

horsel (HOHRSS-el) — a hybrid animal that is part horse and part camel; used as a work animal on Mars

gyrvel (guhr-VEL) — Nabian word meaning "welcome"

Mars Cycle (MARS SY-kuhl) — the Martian year, equal to 687 Earth days, or 1.9 Earth years

matekap (MAH-the-kap) — Nabian word meaning "sleepover"

Nabian (NAY-bee-uhn) — an advanced alien race with nose ridges and plastic-like hair; their eye color reflects their surroundings

Nabia sia carnti (NAY-bee-uh SEE-uh karn-TIE) — Nabian words meaning "my Nabian friend"

Protector (proh-TEK-tohr) — a large silver and black robot that works to enforce the laws of Mars

pwenthar karaal (pwen-THAR ka-RAHL) — Nabian words meaning "shape-shifter"

sol (SOHL) — the name for the Martian day

Sulux (SUH-lux) — an alien race with purple skin and arm and neck ridges

talazin parthenax (tal-uh-ZEEN PARTH-uh-nacks) — Nabian word for "refugee"

turken (TUR-ken) — a hybrid bird that is part turkey and part chicken; farmers on Mars raise them for their eggs and meat

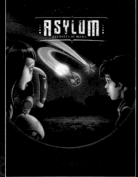